wanisinwak iskwêsisak
awâsisasinahikanis

Two Little Girls Lost in the Bush
A Cree Story for Children

Told by Nêhiyaw / Glecia Bear
Edited and Translated by Freda Ahenakew & H.C. Wolfart
Illustrated by Jerry Whitehead

Fifth House Publishers
Saskatoon Saskatchewan

Canadian Cataloguing in Publication Data

Bear, Glecia, 1912–

    Wanisinwak iskwêsisak – Two little girls lost in the bush

    Text in Cree and English.
    ISBN 0–920079-77-6

I. Ahenakew, Freda, 1932–   II. Wolfart, H. Christoph, 1943–
III. Whitehead, Jerry.   IV. Title.   V. Title: Two little girls lost in the bush.

E99.C88B42   1991   jC897.3   C91–097191-9

This book has been published with the assistance
of The Saskatchewan Arts Board, The Canada Council and The Secretary of State.

Fifth House Publishers
620 Duchess Street
Saskatoon, Saskatchewan S7K 0R1

Printed in Canada.

PREFACE

I want to thank my aunt Nêhiyaw / Glecia Bear who gave me this story in the hope that it will give pleasure to our grandchildren and great-grandchildren, and that they may also see it as an example of self-reliance.

The original text of this story is part of a larger collection of women's life experiences, to be published in Cree with an English translation, under the title

kôhkominawak otâcimowiniwâwa / Our Grandmothers' Lives, As Told in Their Own Words

Edited and Translated by Freda Ahenakew & H.C. Wolfart,
Fifth House Publishers, Saskatoon, Saskatchewan

The story was recorded, and the printed text was prepared from the tape recording and then translated, with the support of the Social Sciences and Humanities Research Council of Canada and the Cree Language Project at the University of Manitoba.

The illustrations were commissioned and printed with the support of a grant from the Department of the Secretary of State to the First Nations Women Writers.

F.A. (& H.C.W.)

INTRODUCTION

This story was told to me by my aunt, and it is a true story. She herself experienced it, along with her little sister, when they were eleven and eight years old. Now many of her great-grandchildren are about that age, and she is seventy-eight.

Her friends and relatives call her *Nêhiyaw*; others know her as Glecia Bear. She lives at *paskwâwi-sâkahikanihk* / Meadow Lake in northern Saskatchewan, and this is where she raised eleven children of her own and many other children and grandchildren.

She was born and raised at *kwâkopîwi-sâkahikanihk* / Green Lake, which today is less than an hour away by car; but at the time she got married and moved, it must have taken the better part of a day with a team of horses. Her younger sister Gigi still lives at Green Lake.

In this story, Nêhiyaw tells us about a real experience: although she was only eleven years old, she was already given a big responsibility. When people had only a few cows, to watch over one of them at calving time was an important assignment. And to follow it into the densely forested wilderness was a serious task.

She was still a child, ready to play when the chance arose, but at the same time mature enough to deal with a crisis.

When the cow got stuck and the two little girls realised they were lost, she took charge and proved herself remarkably levelheaded and resourceful, seeking shelter from the rain under a spruce and using her clothes to wrap up her sister's bare feet, and also to keep her warm. Nêhiyaw had been on her way back from church and was still wearing sturdy shoes with her Sunday best.

The community's response to the crisis was equally remarkable. All segments of the community took part in the search: men and women, hunters experienced in tracking and with expertise in conducting a search, the Roman Catholic priest leading the prayers, and the Hudson's Bay Company manager providing the gear — and, in the end, new clothes for the two little girls.

The high point of the story comes when the little girl realises that the strange noises of the owl and its flapping wings are no cause for fear but a signal of hope: although many Cree people are afraid of owls and see them as bearers of bad news, owls may also offer help and guidance.

nisîmis awa, *'Gigi'* isiyîhkâsow, kwâkopîwi-sâkahikanihk, ayinânêw ê-itahtopiponêt, pêyakosâp niya ê-itahtopiponêyân. êkwa nikî-nitawi-ayamihân êwako anima kîkisêpâ ê-nitawi-saskamoyân, nimâmâ awa ê-wîcêwak ê-nitawi-saskamoyân anima. ê-pê-kîwêyâhk êkwa, nipâpâ êkwa – nikî-wîhtamâkonân sâsay, otâkosihk isi ê-wîhtamâkoyâhk, mostos awa ê-wî-otawâsimisit nânitaw ôtê sakâhk; êkwa, "aswahohk!" itwêw, "atisamânihk;" (kayâs mâna kî-atisamânihkêwak êkota mostoswak ê-asikâpawicik), "asawâpamihk êwako ana onîcâniw!" itwêw, "sêskisici, pimitisahwâhkêk!" nititik awa nipâpâ; "ka-pimitisahwâwâw, mâka êkâya cîki ohci ka-pimitisahwâyêk, nâh-nakîci, ka-kiskêyihtam ê-pimitisahwâyêk, piko wâhyawês ohci piko ka-pimitisahwâyêk, êkâ ka-wâpamikoyêk," itwêw.

My little sister is called *Gigi*, we lived at Green Lake, she was eight years old, and I, I was eleven years old. And I had been to church early that morning to take communion, I had gone with my mom to take communion. On our way home, my dad — he had told us, telling us the previous evening already, that one cow would be calving somewhere in the bush over here; so he had said, "Watch out for her at the smudge!" (they used to make smudges long ago, with the cows standing about there), "Look out for that female!" he had said, "When she goes into the bush, then you all follow her!" my dad had said to me; "you follow her, but you should not follow her too closely, for when she stops now and then, she will know that you are following her, you have to follow her from a little distance, so that she will not see you," he had said.

êkwa ôma, mwêhci êkwa ê-pê-takosiniyâhk awa nimâmâ, ayamihêwikamikohk ohci ê-pê-takohtêyâhk, mostos awa, tâpwê ôho nipâpâ kâ-kî-itwêt kâ-asawâpamâyâhk, mwêhci kâ-pimi-sipwêhtêt ana mostos, ây, êy, kwayas tôhtôsâpoy ayâw; ê-wî-ati-sêskisit. tâpwê piko êkwa kâ-pîhtikwêpahtâyân êkwa nêtê aya, ê-wîsâmak ana nisîmis. "wîcêwin," nititâw awa, "ka-nitawi-pimitisahwâyahk ana mostos!" nititâw — nipapâsimâw, sâsâkihtiw, êkosi isi, môya wâhyaw êtokwê ê-itêyihtamâhk ayis. sâsâkihtiw, niya wiya kêyâpic nipohtiskên nicayiwinisisa ôma kâ-kî-nitawi-saskamoyân. mâka môya nimîcison, êkwa ayi — kayâs ayis mâna, piko môya ka-mîcisoyan, kâ-âcimisoyan ka-saskamoyan, môya tâpiskôc anohc. kikî-ocihcihkwanapin ê-saskamonahikawiyan ayamihêwikamikohk, anohc êkwa kinîpawin, kicihcîhk êkwa kimiyikawin êkwa saskamowin, ê-saskamonahisoyan; mîna môya ayamihêwiyiniw, konita êkwa ayisiyiniw kitati-saskamonahik; mistahi pîtos ahpô êwako anima êkwa anohc ayamihâwin kâ-ay-ispayik. kîkwây êtokwê ka-kî-tâpwêwakêyihtamihk, pahkw-âyamihâwin ahpô môniyâwi-ayamihâwina êkwa ôma anohc kâ-ispayik; kayâs kî-kihcêyihcikâtêw pahkw-âyamihâwin. tâsipwâw wiya niya kêyâpic êwako ê-pimitisahamân misakâmê; kîkwây ninîkihikwak kâ-kî-kiskinahamawicik, môya wîhkâc ka-kî-pakitinamân, êkosi ka-isi-nakataskêyân, kîkwây kâ-kî-nakatamawicik.

êkosi êkwa, kâ-sipwêhtêyâhk awa nisîmis awa, nipimitisahok, tâpwê nipâpâ kâ-kî-itwêt, "wâhyaw ohci pimitisahohk!" kâ-itwêt. mayaw ana kâ-wî-nakît mostos, êkosi mâna ê-kî-nawakipayihoyâhk ê-apiyâhk; têpiyâhk ê-ati-wâpamâyâhk ê-ati-nôkosit, tânitê kâ-itohtêt.

And then, just as we were getting home, my mom and I, as we were arriving home from church, at that moment the cow, the very one for which my dad had told us to look out, was going off, wow, hey, she had lots of milk; she was heading into the bush. So I straight away ran inside over there and asked my little sister along. "Come with me," I said to her, "to follow that cow!" I said to her − I rushed her, she was barefoot but came like that, for we did not think it would be far. She was barefoot but I, I still wore the clothes in which I had gone to  communion. But I had not eaten − for in the old days you had to fast before you went to confession and communion, not like today. You used to kneel in church when you were given communion, whereas today you stand and the host is put in your hand and you put it in your mouth yourself; also, it is not the priest but an ordinary person who is giving you communion; things are done very differently in church today. I do not know what one should believe, the Catholic Church or the White-Man's religions and what is going on today; in the old days, the Catholic Church was highly thought of. In fact, I myself still follow it all the way; what my parents had taught me, I would never let that go, and I will die with what my parents have left to me.

And so we took off, with my little sister following me, exactly as my dad had said, "Follow her from a distance!" he had said. As soon as the cow was about to come to a halt, we would duck down and stay there; so long as we continued to keep her in view to see where she was going.

wahwâ, kêtahtawê êkotê ê-takohtêyâhk, pôti awa ôtê kî-pimicikâpawiw awa (kinwês mâka ê-pimohtêyâhk, mitoni wâhyaw anima êtokwê ê-ocawâsimisit), êkotê kâ-pimicikâpawit ê-nôhâwasot. wahwâ, êkwa ani kâ-itohtêyâhk, wah, nimôcikêyihtênân êkotê, wahwâ, moscosos awa ê-nônic awa.

Oh my, as we arrived over there, all at once there she stood sideways (but we had walked a long way, it must have been far off where she had her calf), there she stood sideways, suckling her calf. Oh my, and now we went over there, oh, we were excited; oh my, the little calf was sucking.

nipakwahcêhonis awa, nisîpêkiskâwasâkâs ohci, *belt* ana kâ-tahkopitak okwayâhk, awa nisîmis êkwa êkoni ê-miciminât; êkwa niya ê-îkinak ana mostos, iyikohk mistahi tôhtôsâpoy ê-ayât; konita ê-pâh-pâhpiyâhk êkota, ê-mêtawâkêyâhk anima tôhtôsâpoy, ê-âh-îkinamawak awa nisîmis wîhkwâkanihk. ê-kî-sîkopitimâyâhk êkwa anihi otôhtôsima awa mostos êkwa, nitahkitisahwâw êkwa. tâpwê êkwa kâ-sipwêhtêt, nitati-askowânân awa moscosos ê-pimitisahwât, nêsowisiw awa moscosos awa.

When I had tied it fast with my belt, from my sweater, around its neck, then my little sister held the calf; and then I, I milked the cow, she had so much milk; we just kept laughing, then, as we played with the milk, with me squirting it on my little sister's face. When we had drained the milk from her teats, I drove the cow forward. And, indeed, she started walking, with us following behind the calf as it followed her, the calf was quite weak.

wahwâ, kêtahtawê êkwa, sîpîsis ê-pimihtik, êkota êkwa ana mostos êkwa môya wî-âsowaham ana. kâ-pasastêhwak êkwa ana mostos, êkwa ê-pâhkopêtisahwâyâhk êkwa (tâpwê piko, êcika ani itê ê-tastôstôkahk anima), kâ-ati-kotâwipayit ana mostos, ê-waskawît tahki ayiwâk ê-ati-kotâwipayit, ana mostos. êkosi isi êkwa, moscosos ana êkwa, ana ita ana kâ-tahkopitât anima nipakwahtêhon ohci − moscosos ana kâ-tahkopitak êkwa êkota, sakâhk êkota, nitahkopitâw. êkosi êkwa ê-wî-nitawi-wîhtamâhk, awa mostos awa êkwa ê-ati-kotâwipayit awa; aspin âta wiya âpihtaw kêyâpic ê-nôkosit, êkwa kâ-sipwêhtêyâhk.

Oh my, after a while there ran a creek, and there now the cow refused to cross. Then I whipped her and we chased her into the water (as it turned out, in fact, into a bog), and then the cow began sinking into it, and as she moved she began to sink in deeper and deeper. So now, as my little sister had tied the calf around the neck with my belt − with that belt I tied the calf up, I tied it up there in the bush. So now we were about to go and tell about the cow sinking in; from the distance, half of her could still be seen when we left.

êcika ani êkwa, êkosi êkwa ê-wanisiniyâhk. êkwa sâsay ôma ê-ati-takwâkik kâ-tâh-tahkâyâk ati. wahwahwâ, êkwa ani kâ-pimohtêyâhk kâ-pimohtêyâhk, ê-mâtot awa nisîmis, êkwa niya ê-têpwêyân ê-têpwêyân nîsta, ka-kakwê-pêhtâkawiyâhk. êy, ê-sâ-sêkwâhtawîyâhk ita ê-kâh-kawisihkik ôkik minahikwak, ita kâ-cawâsik ê-sîpâhtawîyâhk mâna ê-pimohtêyâhk.

And with that, as it turned out, we were lost. It was already early fall, when it begins to get cold. Oh my oh my, and now we walked and walked, and my little sister was crying, and I myself was yelling and yelling so that we might be heard. Hey, we were crawling under fallen spruce-trees, we would crawl through underneath, where there was a little opening, as we went along.

piyis êkwa ê-tipiskâk êkwa, ôh, êkwa ani êkwa kâ-kimiwahk. sîpâ êkwa minahikohk, âsay mitoni nisikwâskocininân; sîpâ êkwa minahikohk êkwa kâ-apiyân êkwa ayi, misi-minahik awa, êkota êkwa ê-apiyân, êkwa awa anima nisîpêkiskâwasâkâs, ôta ê-tahkonak awa nisîmis ê-nawakapiyân, ê-akwanahak êkwa êkota ê-wî-kakwê-kîsônak ôma, kanakê wiya ka-kîsôsit. kapê-tipisk êkosi êkota êkwa, tâpwê nipâw, nîsta ninipân. ê-wî-wa-waniskâyâhk, ôh, kwayas pâh-pâkisitêpayiw ê-kîskicihk awa nisîmis awa. êkwa kayâs maskimotêkin ayis piko kikî-wiyâhtên − êkotowa pîhtawêsâkân, sîhcâskwahonis, kitôhtôsimak êkocowa ohci maskimotêkin ê-kî-osîhtâhk, êkotowa piko kikî-wiyâhtên. êkwa, kâ-itak êkwa ana nisîmis, "nipîhtawêsâkân ôma nika-kêcikonên, nika-titipahpitên kisita," nititâw. tâpwê êkwa kâ-kêcikonamân anima nipîhtawêsâkân, nitâskipitên âpihtaw, niwâh-wêwêkahpitâw êkwa, osita, êwako ohci anima.

At last it was night, oh, and now it rained. So then I sat under a spruce-tree, our clothes were already quite torn by the branches; sitting under a spruce-tree, it was a big spruce-tree where I sat, there I held my little sister, huddled over her and covering her with my sweater so as to keep her warm, so that she, at least, would be warm. All night we were there like that, and she did indeed sleep, and I slept too. As we were waking up, oh, my little sister had badly swollen feet since she had cut herself. And in the old days, of course, all you had to wear was flour-sacking — slips made from that kind, and the brassiere for your breasts was also made from that kind, from flour-sacks, that kind was all you had to wear. Then I said to my little sister, "I will take off my slip and bind your feet with it," I said to her. And so I took off my slip and tore it in half and then wrapped her feet up with it.

âsay mîna êkwa kâ-sipwêhtêyâhk êkwa, nipimohtânân kapê-kisik, iyikohk âsay mîna kâ-pimohtêyâhk. ma kîkway ê-mîciyâhk, nistam kâ-tipiskâk anima kâ-ati-otâkosik ninôhtêhkatânân; ê-nôhtê-minihkwêt awa nisîmis, maskêkohk wiya mâna kâ-otihtamâhk, ê-wâtihkêyân isko nipiy ka-miskamân, êkwa mâna nicihciy ohci ê-minahak anima nipiy. êkosi mâna nisipwêyâcihonân kâwi.

wâ, piyis êkwa sôskwâc êkwa ayi, sâ-sikohtatâw anihi, mîna mâna âhtahpitamân anima, nipîhcawêsâkânis anima ohci, osita kâ-titipahpitamwak, mêscihtatâw. êkwa êwako ôma êkwa nisîhcâskwahonis êkwa (nitôhtôsimihk anima ohci êkwa ani, *my brassiere* âhk-îtâp êtokwê anima), êwako ani anima êkwa ohci êkwa mîna kâ-titipahpitak, âpihtaw êkwa êwako anima mîna ê-tâskipitamân ê-wêwêkahpitamwak, katiskaw wanaskoc ôtê ôho osicisa. â, môya kinwês mêstâskocihcâw, wanihtâw anima pêyak ê-manâskocihtât. "môya êkwa niwî-pimohtân ayiwâk," nititik. êkosi ê-mâtot iyikohk, piyis môya ahpô ê-pêhtâkosit, iyikohk ê-mâh-mâtot ahpô.

So now we left again, walking all day, and again we walked so much. We had nothing to eat, and the first night we felt hungry, towards evening; as my sister wanted to drink, I dug a hole when we reached a muskeg until I found water, and then gave her water to drink with my cupped hands. And so we would travel on some more.

Well, at last she simply wore out the rags on her feet, and I changed the bandages, binding her feet with my little slip, she had worn them out completely. And now I used my brassiere (the cloth from my breasts, it was much like a bra), now I also used that to bandage her again, tearing it in half and wrapping it around her little feet, barely covering the tips. Well, it was not long before, being in the bush, she had none of that left, also having lost one by getting it caught. "Now I am not going to walk any further," she said to me. And with that she cried so much that, finally, she could not even be heard any more, so much had she been crying.

kâ-nayômak êkwa; nîsta wiya ninêstosin; êkwa misikitiw anima êkwayikohk, ayinânêw ê-itahtopiponêt êkwa ê-kî-wiyinot. kâ-nayômak êkwa, ê-pimohtêyân ê-pimohtêyân, ê-nayômak. â, âsay mîna êkwa ê-tipiskâk, âsay mîna êkwa minahik, âsay mîna ninitonawâw, sêkwâ-ayihk êkota ka-ayâyâhk. êkota êkwa sêkwâ-ayihk êkwa ê-ayâyâhk, wâcistakâc, kâ-wâh-wâsaskotêpayik êkwa, iyikohk ê-maci-kîsikâk êkosi anima êwako anima tipiskâw. mâka môya nisâpopânân, minahikohk ayis sîpâ nitayânân, mâka sâpopêwa wiya nitayiwinisinâna anima kâ-pimohtêyâhk, âh? êkota êkwa sîpâ êkwa, âsay mîna kâ-apiyân, âsay mîna pêyakwan, ê-cahkonak awa nisîmis, â, sîpêkiskâwasâkâs anima, wâcistakâc, sikwâskocin. êwako ani anima êkwa, âsay mîna ohci êkwa, wiya êkwa niya êkwa nama kîkway nitâpacihtân, wiya êkwa niwêwêkinâw êkota, âsay mîna nipâw, wiya ê-nêstosit. nîsta ninipân; ê-ati-wâpahk, kêtahtawê kâ-pêhtawak ôhow ê-kâh-kitot êkota, tahkohc êkota minahikohk. ê-koskopayit, koskomik awa wîsta nisîmis, sêmâk mâtow, "ê-wî-nôtinikoyahk," ê-itwêt ôho, otahtahkwana ôho mâna anisi isi ê-taswêkiwêpinât awa ôhow. nîsta êkosi nititêyihtên, ê-pê-itâpit mâna anima ita kâ-apiyâhk.

I carried her on my back now; but I, too, was tired; and she was quite big, she was eight and she used to be fat. I carried her on my back now, walking and walking and carrying her on my back. Well, and again it was night, and again I looked for a spruce-tree for us to stay underneath there. There we stayed, underneath, oh my God, there was lightning now, it was such a bad storm that night. But we did not get wet for we were beneath a spruce-tree, but our clothes got wet when we were walking, eh? And again I sat underneath there, the same thing again, holding my little sister, well, with that little sweater, oh my God, she was torn ragged. And again I used that one, I had nothing to use for myself, but I wrapped her up with that, and again she fell asleep for she was tired. I slept too; towards dawn, suddenly I heard an owl hooting there, on that spruce-tree above. My little sister woke up, the owl woke her up, too, and she started crying right away, "It is going to attack us," she said about it, as the owl would flap its wings like that [gesture]. I thought so, too, as it looked at us where we sat.

well, "kika-sipwêhtânaw," nititâw awa nisîmis; âsay mîna, nisipwêhtânân. âsay mâka mîna ê-nayômak ôma êkwa, sâsay mîna ê-sipwêhtêyâhk. wiya iyikohk ê-pâkisitêpayit, nîsta wiya nisikwâskocinin niskâtihk misiwê, mâka niya wiya miscikwaskisinisa nikî-kikiskên êkospî. êkwa ani êkwa, awa ôhow êkwa, mayaw ê-sipwêhtêyâhk, tâpwê piko kâ-sipwêpihât; wâhyawês mitoni nêtê êkwa, mîtosihk êkwa nêtê kâ-akosît. kâ-pê-kwêsk-âyât, êkosi isi anima, otahtahkwana mâna anisi isi ê-isi-wêpinât, pâskac ê-pêhtâkosit kisik, ê-taswêkiwêpinât, tâpiskôc ê-wî-nôtinikoyâhk. cîki ê-ati-ayâyâhk, sâsay mîna kâ-sipwêpihât, sâsay mîna êkotê êkwa minahikohk akosîw. pêyakwan êkosi, itêhkê isi ôma kâ-ayâyâhk pê-itâpiw, êkosi anima mâna ê-itôtahk, ê-pêhtâkosit. "wahwâ," kâ-itak awa nisîmis, "ka-pimitisahwânaw awa," nititâw, "ahpô êtokwê awa ê-wî-kiskinohtahikoyâhk awa, kâ-itôtahk," nititâw. "namôya!" itwêw, "ê-wî-nôtinikoyahk ana, kâ-itôtahk," itwêw awa nisîmis, "môya kika-pimitisahwânaw," itwêw. "môya," nititâw, "ka-pimitisahwânaw mahti," nititâw.

Well, "We will leave," I said to my little sister; and again we left. But I was again carrying her on my back, as we left again. Her feet were so swollen and I, too, had cuts all over my legs but I wore oxfords that day. And now, indeed, as soon as we left, straight away the owl also flew off; landing on a tree over there, quite a distance ahead of us. It turned to face us, in the same way as before, moving its wings like that [*gesture*] and, on top of it all, making strange noises at the same time and flapping its wings as if it were going to attack us. When we got close, again it flew off, again landing on a spruce-tree over there. In the same manner, it looked towards where we were, doing the same thing, making strange noises. "Oh my," I said to my little sister, "we will follow it," I said to her, "maybe it is going to show us the way when it does that," I said to her. "No!" she said, "it is going to attack us when it does that," said my little sister, "we will not follow it," she said. "No," I said to her, "we will follow it and see," I said to her.

tâpwê êkwa, kâ-pimitisahwâyâhk, âsay mîna êkosi ana ôhow. nânitaw êtokwê anima nêwâw ê-âhci-twêhot ana ôhow mâna, êkwa nipimitisahwânân êkwa. *boy*, kêtahtawê kâ-pêhtamân tâpiskôc awiyak ê-têpwêt. nitêpwân, mâka ayis nimiyiskwân, môya êkwayikohk nikisîwân. pêhtamwak mâka êsa anikik, *'Alec Bishop'* ana kî-isiyîhkâsow, *Louis Morin, Salamon Morin*, êkwa *Johnny Sinclair*. êcika ani ê-itasiwêcik, nâh-nêwo, ê-wî-nâh-nêwicik ôkik nâpêwak; *Hudson's Bay store* ohci ê-miyihcik pâskisikana, môsosiniya, *rubbers*, ê-miyihcik ka-nitonâkoyâhkwâw; kapê-ayi ôma êsa ê-nitonâkoyâhkwâw anima nistam kâ-wanisiniyâhk, nistam anima kâ-kîsikâk. nîkân êsa misiwê kî-papâmipayiwak, ê-papâmi-nitonâkawiyâhk wâskahikanihk ôma, âh? êkosi êkwa kiskêyihtamwak êkwa ayi, ê-wanisiniyâhk.

And indeed we again followed the owl, in the same way. It must have changed its perch about four times, and we followed it. *Boy*, all at once it seemed as if I heard someone yelling. I yelled but, of course, my voice was weak, I was not loud enough. But they heard it, Alec Bishop was his name, and Louis Morin, Salamon Morin and Johnny Sinclair. It appears they had planned teams of four, these men would go in fours; they had been given guns, shells and rubber overshoes by the Hudson's Bay store to search for us; they had been searching for us all the time since first we had got lost, since that first day. First of all they had gone around everywhere on horseback, looking for us in all the houses, eh? and then they knew that we were lost.

êkosi anima êsa, êkâ kî-nakatâyâhk ana mostos anima ita kâ-micimoskowêt anima, kâ-ati-kotâwipayit anima,

(*David Merasty*, ominahowiyiniw, êwako ana êsa, kî-masinahikêhâw êwako ana ê-mitihtikoyâhk, âh? mâka êkwa niwanahâhtikonân, îh! anima iyikohk kâ-kimiwahk, â, môya piyis êtokwê nôkwan ôma ita kâ-pimohtêyâhk, nikî-mitihtikonân wiya — tâsipwâw kî-nitawi-miskawêw anihi mostoswa. ôtê isko okwayâhk, ana mostos êkwa sâsay — mâka kêyâpic ê-pimâtisit, pê-wîhtam êsa êkwa, nêtê kwâkopîwi-sâkahikanihk ê-miskawât anihi mostoswa; nipâpâwa êkwa ê-pê-wîhtamawât. êkosi nipâpâ mêkiw, anihi mostoswa ka-pê-pâskisomiht; êkosi kî-pê-nipahêwak anihi mostoswa, anihi mîna moscososa.)

nikâh-kî-miskâkawinân êwako tipiskâw, *lanterns* ê-miyihcik êsa, kahkiyaw ôkik nâpêwak *Hudson's Bay* ohci ê-ohcîstamâhcik, ê-âpacihtâcik *lanterns* ôho, âh? — kayâs êkamâ kîkway *flashlights*. êkwa ôkik êkwa kâ-pêhtawâyâhkik, awa êkwa kâ-matwê-têpwêt, sêmâk nikiskêyihtên, nâpêw êkwa, âha.

If we had not left that cow where she got stuck in the bog, where she was sinking in,

(David Merasty, a hunter, had been hired to track us, eh? but lost our tracks, look! because it had rained so much, well, finally our tracks were no longer visible, I guess, but he had tracked us — as a matter of fact, he had gone and found the cow. She had already sunk in up to her neck but she was still alive, he went back over there to Green Lake to tell that he had found the cow; he came back to tell my dad about it. So my dad gave the cow up to be shot; and they came and killed that cow, and also the calf.)

we would have been found the same night, they were given lanterns, all the men were provided with lanterns from the Hudson's Bay store to use, eh? — there were no flashlights in the old days. And those whom we now heard, the one who was yelling now, I knew right away that now it was a man [not an animal], yes.

êkwa êsa itwêw awa êkwa, wâpikwayâs, *Louis* wâpikwayâs, "ta-tapasîwak ahpô êtokwê," itwêw êsa, "anisi isi ka-wâskâhtêwak ôkik nâpêwak, ôma itê tâpiskôc kâ-pêhtawâyâhkwâw, ka-tapasîwak nânitaw isi, kostahkwâwi, kotak ayisiyiniw kîkway itêyihtahkwâwi," itwêw awa. êkosi êsa êkwa awa pêyak êkwa pê-taskamohtêw êkwa, ê-pê-nâtikoyâhk, itê isi kâ-pêhtâkoyâhk. ê-matwê-têpwêt, â, êkwa mitoni nikêhcinâhon êkwa ayisiyiniw, "kimiskâkawinaw," nititâw awa nisîmis. nitêpwân, mâka ayis nikohtaskway, kâ-pê-sâkêwêt êkota *Alec Bishop*. tâpwê piko ê-pê-wâh-otihtinikoyâhk ê-mâtot, ê-wâh-ocêmikoyâhk awa kisêyinîsis — môya, êkospî osk-âyiwiw, môya kisêyinîwiw.

And *wâpikwayâs*, Louis *wâpikwayâs* had said, "They may even run away," he had said, "let the men go around that way [*gesture*], over here where we think we have heard them, just in case they run away if they get scared and think it might be some strange person," he had said. And so one man had come straight across towards us to come and fetch us, towards where they had heard us. He could be heard yelling, well, and now I knew for certain that it was a human being, "We have been found," I said to my little sister. I yelled but, of course, my throat was weak, then Alec Bishop came into view there. Straight away he came and grabbed both of us and cried, he kissed both of us, this old man — no, he was young then, he was not an old man.

êkosi tâpwê piko êkwa pâskisikan anima kâ-tahkonahk, nistwâw matwêwêhtâw. êkosi anikik môya kinwês ôkik kâ-wâskâhtêcik, êkota pê-takopahtâwak. pâh-pêyak mistatimwa mîna miyâwak, mîciwin ê-pimohtatâcik êkota, môsosiniya, kahkiyaw kîkway, âh? wîstawâw ka-mîcisocik êkwa miskâkawiyâhki ka-piminawatikawiyâhk. êkosi êkwa êkota, sêmâk awa êkwa kotawêw *Louis* wâpikwayâs, ka-kakwê-mîcisoyâhk. ôh, môya kinwês, âsay misiwê kâ-matwêwêhtâhk, awa êkwa kâ-matwêwêhtât, misiwê itê konita kâ-pêhtâkwahki êkwa, ôkik kîkway wîstawâw ê-miskâkawiyâhk ka-kiskêyihtâkwahk, misiwê matwêwêhtâwak. êkosi êkwa, êkota êkwa, *tea* êkwa niwî-minahikawinân ka-mîcisoyâhk, êy, kahkiyaw kîkway, *Hudson's Bay* wiya ohci sôskwâc mîciwin ê-mêkihk. môya nikaskihtânân ahpô ka-kohcipayihtâyâhk anima, *tea* anima, namôya nikî-mîcisonân, mwâc sôskwâc!

And so, with the gun which he carried, he straight away shot three times. So it was not long before the others, who had gone around, came running there. Each of them had also been given a horse to ride, they carried food, shells and everything, eh? for themselves to eat and to cook for us when we would be found. So then Louis *wâpikwayâs* right away made a fire so that we could try to eat. Oh, and it was not long before shots were fired all over, when he had fired his shots, shooting was now heard just everywhere, so that it would be known to these people, too, that we had been found, they were firing shots all over. So then they were going to give us tea to drink there, so that we might eat, hey, everything, for the food had simply been given out by the Hudson's Bay. We were not even able to swallow the tea, we certainly could not eat at all!

êkosi êkwa, êkwa *Louis* wâpikwayâs êkwa itwêw, ka-têhtapiyâhk êkwa niyanân, êkwa ana mistatim ê-sakâpêkinâcik nitêhtapinân êkwa ê-kîwêhtahikawiyâhk êkwa. nêtê êkwa ê-takosiniyâhk, êkwa nîkinâhk êkwa, ayi (— kani tâpwê awa ôhow, ispî êkwa kâ-miskâkoyâhkik ôkik, ana êkwa ôhow, aspin ê-sipwêpihât, ana ôhow, êwako ana ê-kiskinohtahikoyâhk). nêtê êkwa nîkinâhk êkwa ê-takosiniyâhk êkwa ê-sâkêwêyâhk êkwa, wâcistakâc mistatimwak, sôskwâc êkwa ê-ihtasit kwâkopîwi-sâkahikanihk ayisiyiniw, êkota ê-ayât, sôskwâc mistatimwak konita kâ-ay-itapicik, êkotê anima, *wagons* kiyikaw. êkwa êcika ani mâna kisik ê-ayamihâcik, ayamihêwiyiniw êkota ê-ayât, ôma ka-kakwê-miskâkawiyâhk, êkota sôskwâc ê-ayamihât ayamihêwiyiniw, êkota anima kahkiyaw, ka-kakwê-miskâkawiyâhk.

So then Louis *wâpikwayâs* said that we would ride on horseback, and we rode as they led the horse and we were taken home. Then, as we arrived over there at our house (— I forgot, this owl truly just flew away, that owl, once we had been found by these men, it was that owl that showed us the way home). As we arrived over there at our house and came into view, oh my God the horses, simply everybody in Green Lake was there, there simply were horses everywhere, and also wagons. They had apparently been praying all the while, with the priest there, that we might be found, the priest and everyone else had simply been praying there that we might be found.

ê-sâkêwêyâhk êkwa, anima nêta, wiya niya sâsay ê-oskinîkiskwêsisiwiyân, "môya niwî-itohtân niya êkotê," nititâw awa *Alec Bishop*, "iyikohk kâ-sikwâskociniyân," nititâw. "êy, êkâya nânitaw itêyihta, *my girl*," nititik *Alec Bishop*, "iyikohk ka-miywêyihtâkwahk ê-miskâkawiyêk," itwêw, "mistahi ôma ê-kitimâkêyimohk ôma," itwêw, "êkâya kîkway nêpêwisiwin kikiskâkok!" itwêw, "kitakohtahitinân." êy, *boy*, êkotê ê-takohtêyâhk, konita ayisiyiniwak kâ-ocêmikoyâhkwâw. '*Frank Séguin*' kî-isiyîhkâsow *Hudson's Bay store*, wêmistikôsiw, êwako ana konita ê-pê-âkwaskitinikoyâhk ê-mâtot; êkosi êkwa, itwêw awa *Frank Séguin*, ayihk aya, "ayiwinisa," itwêw, "awiyak ka-pê-nâtam nêtê atâwêwikamikohk kîkway ka-pohtiskahkik," itwêw. tâpwê êkwa, êkotê êkwa itohtêw êkwa, awa kâ-kî-oyôhkomiyân, ê-nâtahk êkwa kîkway êkota, *Hudson's-Bay*-ayiwinisa, sôskwâc ê-miyikoyâhk ana ê-pohtayiwinisahikoyâhk.

As we came into view now, over there, I of course was a young girl already, "I am not going to go over there," I told Alec Bishop, "with my clothes so torn up," I said to him. "Hey, do not think about it, my girl," Alec Bishop said to me, "there will be such joy that you have been found," he said, "since there was a lot of misery," he said, "do not let modesty get in the way!" he said, "we have brought you back." Hey, boy, and as we arrived over there, all kinds of people were just kissing us. Frank Séguin was the name of the Hudson's Bay store manager, a Frenchman, he came and just hugged us amid tears; and then he said, "As for clothes," he said, "let someone come and fetch something at the store over there for them to wear," he said. And, indeed, my late grandmother went over there and fetched things, Hudson's Bay clothes, he simply gave them to us and fitted us out with clothes.

êkosi êkwa êkota êkwa, sâsay mîna êkwa êkota, êsa ê-kî-piminawasohk êkwa
ê-wî-asamikawiyâhk, ma kîkway, môya niwî-micisonân, môya nikî-mîcisonân,
nikohtaskwânâna ê-wîsakêyihtamâhk. tâpwê piko wiya awa nisîmis awa, nipêwinihk
ê-kî-pimisimiht, êkosi tâpwê piko ê-itihkwâmit, ê-kîsôsimâcik; osita, iyikohk ê-kîskicihk,
akâminakasiya ê-kâh-kêcikwahomâcik; iyikohk ê-kîskicihk osicisa.

êkwa awa nimâmâ ayi, môya kayâs ê-kî-isi-tahkopitâwasot, *Alice Derocher* asici êsa
mâna wîscawâw ê-nîsicik ê-nîso-sipwêhtêcik, âhci piko wîstawâw ê-nitonâkoyâhkwâw;
ê-papâmi-mâtot êsa nimâmâ.

mâcika, êkosi âta wiya ê-kî-miskâkawiyâhk, êkosi êkwa kâh-kîwêwak êkwa,
ê-kî-kîs-âyamihâcik âsay mîna, êkota âsay mîna êkota niya nisaskamonahikawin, mâka
nisîmis wiya mêskwa êkospî ê-ohci-saskamot; nisaskamonahikawin nîsta. êkosi êtokwê
êkwa nîsta êkwa ê-pimisiniyân, êkosi tâpwê piko nîsta kâ-isi-nipâyân; pâtos kîkisêpâ
kâ-ka-koskopayiyân.

So then again now, they had cooked already and we were going to be fed, but we
still would not eat anything, we could not eat as our throats still hurt. And as soon as my
little sister had been put to bed, she fell asleep straight away even as they tucked her in
for warmth; her feet were so cut up, and they pulled the thorns out with a needle; so cut
up were her feet.

And my mom, although she had just recently had a baby, had nevertheless gone out,
together with Alice Derocher, the two of them together, and had searched for us; my
mom crying as they went about.

And now, of course, that we had been found, now the people went home after they
had finished praying again, and then I was again given communion, but my little sister
had not yet had her first communion at that time; I, on the other hand, was given
communion. And I, too, when I lay down, must have fallen asleep immediately; it was
morning before I woke up.

nikî-kakwâtakâcihonân ani; nikî-wâpahtên ê-âyimahk, ayisiyiniw kâ-wanisihk. êkwa
môya wîhkâc ê-ohci-kostâciyâhk ahpô wâkayôs kîkway ka-kostâyâhk, ê-mâmaskâtamân
ê-kaski-tipiskâk kâ-kitocik, kîkway ka-sêkihikoyân, nama kîkway! nama kîkway
ê-ohci-mâmitonêyihtamân. anohc êkwa, nânitaw ka-wanisiniyân, nikâh-nipahi-sêkisin!
nîso-kîsikâw ê-wanisiniyâhk, ôma êkwa aya *next day*, mwêhci anima ê-âpihtâ-kîsikâk
kâ-miskâkawiyâhk.

   êkosi êtokwê.

We really had had a terrible time; I saw how hard it is when a person is lost. And
we never were afraid, we were not even afraid of bears or anything else, and with the
thunder, in the dark of the night, I marvel that I did not think of anything, anything at
all, of which to be scared. If I were to be lost some place today, I would be scared to
death! We were lost for two days, and were found exactly at noon on the third day.

   That is all, I guess.